To our brother and son,
Sarp Ökten.

For further information, contact:
Tumblehome, Inc.
201 Newbury St. #201
Boston, MA 02116, USA
https://tumblehomebooks.org/

ISBN-13 978-1-943431-62-5
ISBN-10 1-943431-62-0
Library of Congress Control Number: 2020943029

Ökten, Arya and Ökten, Giray
The Mathematical Investigations of Dr. O and Arya /
Arya Ökten and Giray Ökten - 1st ed

Illustrations by Chen-Hui Chang
Design by Yu-Yi Ling

Printed in Taiwan

10 9 8 7 6 5 4 3 2 1

# THE MATHEMATICAL INVESTIGATIONS OF DR. O AND ARYA

Arya Ökten and Giray Ökten

# PREFACE

In 2007, Giray taught a math workshop to a group of third, fourth, and fifth graders in Tallahassee, Florida. His audience included his daughter, Arya, and some of her friends. Arya had inherited his love of math and as a result, Giray was always on the lookout for interesting math books to share with her. Unfortunately, although he searched high and low, he was left unsatisfied with the available options. Giray believed that young kids could be taught 'advanced' mathematical topics and that they would enjoy them-- so long as they were presented in the right way. He decided to take matters into his own hands and started teaching workshops in order to introduce Arya, as well as other kids, to interesting mathematics in fun ways.

After experiencing success with his initial workshop in 2007, Giray decided to continue teaching. In the meantime, Arya grew up. After years of watching her father lecture, she became interested in teaching as well. The two of them decided to teach the next workshop together, which was a class on Caesar ciphers (or more simply, secret codes). Making sure that the kids enjoyed the material and had fun during the talk was of critical importance to Giray and Arya. That's when Arya came up with the idea that they should introduce the topic by acting like secret agents, thus incorporating an element of entertainment. The two of them wrote a script, dressed in costume (a pair of dark sunglasses) and taught the class through a series of questions and answers between the two of them. The kids loved the workshop. After quite a few of these co-taught lectures, they decided to write a math book that would be educational while still incorporating the fun and games they developed in the classroom.

Many thanks to Tony Brown, Betsey Brown, and Ai-Ying Choong from Cornerstone Learning Community who hosted Giray's first workshop in 2007, as well as many others afterwards. Thanks to Chen-Hui Chang for turning Arya's sketches into professional cartoons. Thanks to the publishing team from Tumblehome, Rebecca Raibley Bryden, Yu-Yi Ling, and in particular, Barnas Monteith and Penny Noyce who gave a home to the investigations of Dr. O and Arya. Finally, and most importantly, thanks to all the children who participated in our workshops.

# Chapter 1
# SECRET CODES

Let's discuss the "Caesar code with a shift of 1." We start with the alphabet:

ABCDEFGHIJKLMNOPQRSTUVWXYZ

Underneath it, we write the alphabet again, but this time we shift it to the right by one letter:

BCDEFGHIJKLMNOPQRSTUVWXYZA

Notice how A is last, instead of first? We shifted the alphabet and then wrapped the letter A to the end.

It will be good if we write these again, and line them up nicely. That's exactly what Dr. O does!

**Decoding**: Transforming mysterious text (ciphertext) into what it really means (plaintext).

# Challenge:

Can you continue decoding the message **TFDSFU DPEFT** and find the real message?

Decoding **TFDSFU DPEFT**

| | | | | | | | | | | | | | | | | | | | | | | | | | | |
|---|---|---|---|---|---|---|---|---|---|---|---|---|---|---|---|---|---|---|---|---|---|---|---|---|---|---|
| **Plain** | A | B | C | D | **E** | F | G | H | I | J | K | L | M | N | O | P | Q | R | **S** | T | U | V | W | X | Y | Z |
| **Cipher** | B | C | D | E | **F** | G | H | I | J | K | L | M | N | O | P | Q | R | S | **T** | U | V | W | X | Y | Z | A |

Mysterious message: **TFDSFU DPEFT**

Real message: **S E** _ _ _ _ _ _ _ _ _

Answer: The decoded message is: SECRET CODES

TFDSFU DPEFT
↓
SECRET CODES

Yes, I remember now! My plan was to teach a lesson on how to write secret messages!

I get how to decode now, but what if I want to turn plaintext into ciphertext?

It's easy! Just write the plain text in the first row of the table and then find the matching letter in the second row!

 **Encoding**: Transforming plaintext into ciphertext.

How was the plaintext **SECRET CODES** transformed into the ciphertext **TFDSFU DPEFT** in the first place? To transform plaintext into ciphertext, which is called encoding, we will reverse what we did while decoding. We write the alphabet and its shifted version like before.

| Plain | A | B | C | D | **E** | F | G | H | I | J | K | L | M | N | O | P | Q | R | **S** | T | U | V | W | X | Y | Z |
|---|---|---|---|---|---|---|---|---|---|---|---|---|---|---|---|---|---|---|---|---|---|---|---|---|---|---|
| Cipher | B | C | D | E | **F** | G | H | I | J | K | L | M | N | O | P | Q | R | S | **T** | U | V | W | X | Y | Z | A |

Then we place the message **SECRET CODES** in the **Plain** row and find the letter that corresponds to each letter of this message in the **Cipher** row:

SECRET CODES

↓

TFDSFU DPEFT

Can you figure out what Arya's mysterious message to Dr. O is? The answer is at the end of the next page.

**History**[1]

*Both ancient Greeks and Romans thought about how to send secret messages. Greeks had a strange method. They shaved the head of the messenger, and then wrote the message on his head! When the hair grew, they sent the messenger to deliver the message. The recipient shaved his head to read the secret message. Julius Caesar had a more practical solution. He used the method we explained here. He shifted the alphabet by 3 letters to decode and encode.*

[1]Churchhouse, R. F. (2002). Codes and ciphers: Julius Caesar, the Enigma, and the Internet. Cambridge University

Arya's real message to Dr. O on the previous page: Remember to eat lunch

**Making a Code Wheel**[2]

**Code wheels:** A simple way to encode Caesar codes.

**Instructions:**

1. Cut out the circles. Place the smaller circle over the larger circle, and place a paper fastener through the center of both circles.

2. Rotate the smaller circle to the right (clockwise) by the appropriate number of units. To encode a message, replace plaintext letters from the smaller circle with ciphertext letters from the larger circle. To decode, replace ciphertext letters from the larger circle with plaintext letters from the smaller circle.

[2]Caesar Cipher, Doug Schmid, Illuminations, NCTM.

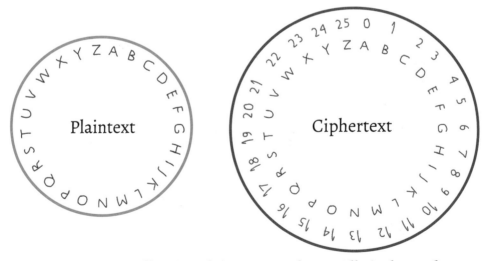

**Attention!** We will write plaintext on the small circle, and ciphertext on the larger circle.

**Exercise:** Decode the previous message of Dr. O using the code wheel:

**TFDSFU DPEFT**

**Solution:** We rotate the small circle clockwise by one letter to obtain the picture below.

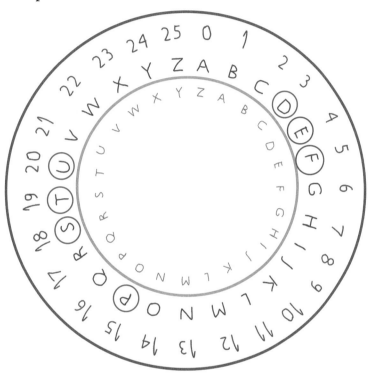

**Remember:** Ciphertext on the bigger circle! You will see the letters of the ciphertext circled.

Now we replace each letter in the ciphertext by the letters they match on the small circle. That gives:

| T | F | D | S | F | U | | D | P | E | F | T |
|---|---|---|---|---|---|---|---|---|---|---|---|
| S | E | C | R | E | T | | C | O | D | E | S |

**Key:** The number of letters we shift the alphabet by while encoding and decoding.

**Exercise:** Encode the message, "There is a cookie in the jar" using a key of 3. (Shift the alphabet by 3.)

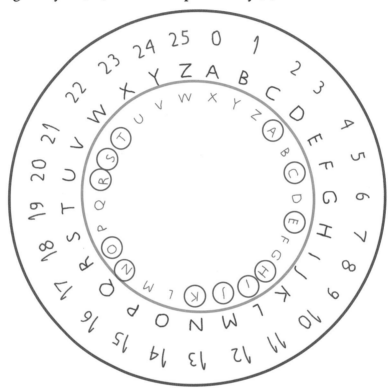

**Solution:** Align the circles in the code wheel so that A on the larger circle matches A on the smaller circle. Then rotate the smaller circle by 3 letters clockwise. Your circle should look like the one above. Next we circle the letters in the plaintext on the small circle. The first letter, T, corresponds to W on the bigger circle. H corresponds to K. Continuing like this, we obtain the ciphertext: **Wkhuh lv d frrnlh lq wkh mdu**.

**Sending messages to a fellow agent!**

1. Write a message to send (no one should see it!).

2. Encode the message using a Caesar code (you should choose a key first).

3. Give the message and the key to your fellow agent.

4. Your fellow agent will decode the message using the key.

## Challenge:

How many different Caesar codes can you find?

**Exercises:**

1. Encode the message "I came. I saw. I conquered.", using a Caesar code with a key of 5. (Do you know who this quote is from?)

2. Decode the message "Eqfkpi ku hwp"

(Hint: A big thinker thinks a Caesar code with a key of 2 was used to create this message!)

# Chapter 2
# NUMBER SOUP

Can you find the sum of the numbers in the soup? But don't try to add them one by one; that would be too boring!

Arya figured out the secret: each pair adds up to 8. If you count how many pairs of numbers there are, you will see that there are three. So the sum of the numbers should be $3 \times 8 = 24$.

**Exercise:** Add numbers 1 through 10.

$$1 + 2 + 3 + 4 + 5 + 6 + 7 + 8 + 9 + 10$$

It is boring to add them one by one! Could we make this problem into a number soup?

**Solution:** Let's pair the numbers as:

1, 10

2, 9

3, 8

4, 7

5, 6

Do you see how each pair adds up to 11? And there are 5 pairs. So the sum of them all is $11 \times 5 = 55$.

*Johann Carl Friedrich Gauss is perhaps the most famous mathematician who ever lived. He was born on April 30, 1777 in Germany. There is a story told about Gauss. When he was in primary school, his teacher had to step out of the classroom for a while, and to keep his students busy, he assigned a difficult problem for them to work on while he was away. Before the teacher could walk out of the classroom, Gauss raised his hand and gave the correct answer! The problem was to find the sum of the numbers 1 through 100, and Gauss solved the problem just like you solved the previous exercise!*

**Exercise:** Add numbers 1 through 7 by pairing them up.

$$1 + 2 + 3 + 4 + 5 + 6 + 7$$

**Solution:** Let's pair

1, 7

2, 6

3, 5

But then, we have one number left, 4, and there is nothing to pair it up with!

No worries: Each of the three pairs above adds up to 8. Therefore their sum is 3×8=24. Now let's add the number 4, which was not included in any of the pairs, to get: 24 + 4 = 28. We are done!

**Adding numbers 1 through 10, Arya's new way:**

Step 1: List the numbers, smallest to largest, and then largest to smallest, aligning them as shown below:

| 1 | 2 | 3 | 4 | 5 | 6 | 7 | 8 | 9 | 10 |
|---|---|---|---|---|---|---|---|---|----|
| 10 | 9 | 8 | 7 | 6 | 5 | 4 | 3 | 2 | 1 |

Step 2: Now add each pair of aligned numbers:

| 1 | 2 | 3 | 4 | 5 | 6 | 7 | 8 | 9 | 10 |
|---|---|---|---|---|---|---|---|---|----|
| 10 | 9 | 8 | 7 | 6 | 5 | 4 | 3 | 2 | 1 |

What is the sum of numbers in each group?

The sum of each group is 11. And there are 10 groups. So that makes a total of 110!

But we solved this problem before and the answer was 55!

Oh no......

Wait, I've got it, look at the groups. Numbers 1-10 are in the first row, and again in the second row. So, we have to divide 110 by 2 for the real final answer: 55!

Brilliant! I like this method, Arya!

Let's solve more problems using this new method!

**Adding numbers 1 through 5:**

Step 1: We first list the numbers.

$$1 \quad 2 \quad 3 \quad 4 \quad 5$$

$$5 \quad 4 \quad 3 \quad 2 \quad 1$$

Step 2: The sum of numbers in each group is 6. There are 5 groups. So the total is:

$$(5×6)÷2 = 30÷2 = 15$$

Look at this, Arya! Look at these solutions. Is there a pattern?

Sum of numbers:

1 through 5 = (5×6) ÷ 2

1 through 7 = (7×8) ÷ 2

1 through 10 = (10×11) ÷ 2

EUREKA! I see a pattern! To find the sum, you just take the last number, times it with the number right after it, and divide the whole thing by two.

Arya found the pattern! It is something like this:

Think about the sum of numbers 1 through some "target number". The target numbers in the problems Dr. O talks about are 5, 7, and 10. Let's write this sum as

$$1 + 2 + 3 + ... + \text{"target number"}$$

The "dots" here mean that we need to keep adding numbers until we reach our "target number". Then the answer is:

$$1 + 2 + 3 + ... + \text{"target number"} = (\text{target number}) \times (\text{the number that comes after the target number}) \div 2$$

Ugh! That's so long and wordy! Can't we simplify? Can we not use the words 'target number"?

Right on, Arya! Mathematicians do this all the time. They use symbols to replace long phrases, and for symbols, they like using letters of the alphabet!

So what can we use for the phrase "target number"?

Let's use "n"! After all, number begins with "n"!

If we do what Dr. O says, then the formula we had before becomes:

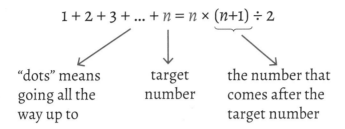

$$1 + 2 + 3 + \ldots + n = n \times (n{+}1) \div 2$$

"dots" means going all the way up to

target number

the number that comes after the target number

Here $n$ replaces the "target number", and ($n$ +1) replaces "the number that comes after the target number." Why ($n$ +1)? Because if we want to find the number that comes after a number, all we need to do is add 1 to it. 6 comes after 5, because 6 = 5 +1. 10 comes after 9, because 10 = 9 +1.

The problem Gauss solved: Remember the problem Gauss' teacher gave to his class? Add numbers 1 through 100. Let's use our formula to solve this problem:

$$1 + 2 + 3 + \ldots + 100 = 100 \times (100{+}1) \div 2$$

$$= 100 \times 101 \div 2 = 10100 \div 2 = 5050$$

Here is how we can add numbers 50 through 100. Let's start with adding numbers 1 through 100, which we did before:

$$1 + 2 + 3 + \ldots + 100 = 5050$$

Now, what do we have to remove from this sum, to get the sum of numbers 50 through 100? Clearly, it is the sum of the numbers from 1 through 49, which we can compute using our formula:

$$1 + 2 + 3 + \ldots + 49 = 49 \times (49 + 1) \div 2 = 49 \times 50 \div 2 = 1225$$

Now take away 1225 from 5050, to get the sum of numbers 50 through 100. It is:

$$5050 - 1225 = 3825.$$

**Exercises:**

1.  Find the sum of numbers 10 through 20.

2.  Find the sum of numbers 20 through 30.

# Chapter 3

# WHAT'S IN AN OPERATION?

## How to Play Krypto[3]:

Each player is given 5 numbers and a target number. Add, subtract, multiply, or divide, using each of the numbers, to obtain the target number.

3. Exploring Krypto, Samuel E. Zordak, Illuminations, NCTM

**Rules:**

1. Every number must be used, and each must be used only once.

2. You can only use addition, subtraction, multiplication, and division.

**Numbers:** 2, 1, 2, 2, 3

**Target:** 20

**Arya's solution:** To keep track of the numbers used in the list of numbers, let's color them. First add 2 and 1 to obtain 3. Then multiply 3 by the 3 from our list, which makes 9. Now multiply 9 by 2, to get 18, and then add 2 to 18, to get the target number 20. Notice how we used all the numbers in our list, and only once! Here is a summary of the calculations:

$$2 + 1 = 3$$

$$3 \times 3 = 9$$

$$9 \times 2 = 18$$

$$18 + 2 = 20$$

Can you find another way to obtain 20 using these numbers?

**Numbers:** 1, 3, 7, 1, 8

**Target:** 1

**Arya's solution:**

$$3 - 1 = 2$$

$$2 + 7 = 9$$

$$9 \div 1 = 9$$

$$9 - 8 = 1$$

**Exercises:**

1.  Numbers: 8, 2, 5, 24, 6

    Target: 4

2.  Numbers: 3, 1, 3, 9, 12

    Target: 14

3.  Numbers: 3, 11, 2, 3, 6

    Target: 10

4.  Numbers: 6, 1, 4, 21, 7

    Target: 4

5.  Numbers: 5, 3, 3, 3, 12

    Target: 9

## Activity — Creating your own Krypto question

1.  Pick five numbers.

2.  Use the numbers and four operations in some arrangement to find a target number.

3.  Give the five numbers and the target number to a friend, and see if they can come up with a solution!

*Arithmetic is the study of numbers and the four basic operations: addition, subtraction, multiplication, and division. Arithmetic was known to ancient Egyptians and Babylonians in 2000 BC. However, the way we do arithmetic today, using numerals 0 through 9, developed much more recently. It was discovered by Indian mathematicians around 400 AD. One thing they realized is that the number zero can be a troublemaker: what happens, for example, if we divide 0 by 0, or 1 by 0? Such questions were raised by Brahmagupta, an Indian mathematician. In the twelfth century, another Indian mathematician, Bhaskara, answered one of these questions and wrote that 1 divided by 0 is an infinite quantity! Today, we can answer such questions using calculus, a subject in mathematics you can learn in high school.*

4. Seife, C. (2000). *Zero: The Biography of a Dangerous Idea.* Penguin Books.

Dr.O, why do we need to have an order of operations?

Great question, Arya! It is because the answer can change depending on the order. For example, think about the calculation 2 + 3 × 5. We can do it in two different ways:

Addition first: 2 + 3 × 5 = 5 × 5 = 25

Multiplication first: 2 + 3 × 5 = 2 + 15 = 17

Well, which one is the right answer, 25 or 17?

If we did not have an order of operations, both answers would be correct, and that would be very confusing! That's why we need an order, so that we have only one answer. Since we choose to have multiplication before addition in the order of operations, the correct answer is 17.

**Inventing a new operation:**

- We need a symbol

- We need to describe the operation

**Example:** Let's use * as our symbol. Here comes our new operation:

$$a * b = a \times (b + 1)$$

Let's make some calculations. How do we compute, 2 * 3? From the way we described *, it should be

$$2 * 3 = 2 \times (3 + 1)$$

where we simply replaced *a* by 2, and *b* by 3. Since $2 \times (3 + 1) = 2 \times 4 = 8$, we have the answer:

$$2 * 3 = 8.$$

Here is another calculation. How about computing 5 * 0 ? Again, from the description of *, we have

$$5 * 0 = 5 \times (0 + 1) = 5 \times 1 = 5.$$

# Challenge:

P, Q represent numbers. P ◉ Q means $(P + Q) \div 2$. What is the value of 3 ◉ (2 ◉ 4)?

(Hint: Remember to do the part in the parenthesis first.)

Does the order matter, when we compute, say, $1 * 2$? Let's see:

$$1 * 2 = 1 \times (2 + 1) = 1 \times 3 = 3$$

$$2 * 1 = 2 \times (1 + 1) = 2 \times 2 = 4$$

So, the order does matter! $1 * 2$ is 3, but $2 * 1$ is 4. We have a special name for operations where order is NOT important.

New word

We say an operation is **commutative**, if the order at which the calculation is done is not important. For example, addition is commutative, since 3 + 5 is the same as 5 + 3, as well as any other numbers you can think of. We can use symbols and write: $a + b = b + a$. Here, by $a$ and $b$, we mean any number you can think of.

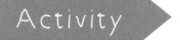

**Activity** > Creating a new operation!

Create an operation. Make sure to find a symbol for your operation and describe it like

$$a \otimes b = ...$$

After you create your operation, answer the following:

1. What is $2 \otimes 3$?

2. Is your operation commutative?

**Another Property of Operations: Identity Property**

What happens when you add zero to a number? It does not change anything! In other words,

$$a + 0 = 0 + a = a.$$

We say 0 is the identity element for addition.

**Identity element for multiplication:** Just like Arya discovered, 1 is the identity element for multiplication. Multiplying a number by 1 does not change anything! We can write this as

$$a \times 1 = 1 \times a = a.$$

# Challenge:

Does * have an identity element? Recall how we defined this operation: $a * b = a \times (b + 1)$

**Playing Krypto with different operations:**

Let's add * to our Krypto game. Can you reach the target using +, *, and ÷ ?

**Example:**

Numbers: 2, 1, 2, 2, 3

Target: 20

**Solution:**

$2 * 3 = 8$

$8 + 2 = 10$

$10 * 2 = 20$

$20 ÷ 1 = 20$

**Exercise:**

Use +, *, and ÷ to reach the target with four numbers.

Numbers: 1, 1, 2, 3

Target: 10

# Chapter 4

# PRIME NUMBERS

We say a number is divisible by another number if the division problem works out to an integer. That is, when we divide one number by the other, we get a whole number (one with no decimal.) What is an integer? The numbers 0, 1, 2, ... as well as their negative versions, -1, -2, -3, ... are the integers.

## Even numbers & Odd numbers

If a number is divisible by 2, then we call it an even number. Even numbers are 0, 2, 4, 6, ... And those numbers which are not divisible by 2 are called odd numbers, such as 1, 3, 5, ...

## DIVISIBILITY RULES

Here is how we can answer Dr. O's questions:

**Dividing by 2:** Even numbers are divisible by 2. To check if a number is even, we just need to look at its last digit. If the last digit is even, then the number is even. For example, 96714 is an even number, because its last digit, 4, is an even number.

**Exercise:** Is 123456 divisible by 2?

**Dividing by 3:** Add up the digits; if the sum is divisible by 3, then the number is too. For example, 273 is divisible by 3, because the sum of the digits of 273 is $2 + 7 + 3 = 12$, and 12 is divisible by 3. In fact, we can use long division to show $273 \div 3 = 91$.

**Exercise:** Is 123456 divisible by 3?

**Dividing by 4:** Look at the last two digits. If they are divisible by 4, then the number is divisible by 4 as well. For example, 39624 is divisible by 4, since its last two digits 24 is divisible by 4!

**Exercise:** Is 123456 divisible by 4?

**Dividing by 5:** If the last digit is a 5 or 0, then the number is divisible by 5. This is easy to check! Numbers 0, 5, 10, 15, 20, 25, ... are the ones that are divisible by 5.

**Dividing by 6:** If the number is divisible by both 2 and 3, then it is divisible by 6.

**Exercise:** Is 123456 divisible by 6?

**Dividing by 9:** Add the digits. If the sum is divisible by 9, then the number is divisible by 9 as well. For example, check out 52866. If we add digits, we get $5 + 2 + 8 + 6 + 6 = 27$. Since 27 is divisible by 9, then the rule says 52866 is also divisible by 9.

**Exercise:** Is 123456 divisible by 9? How about 1234566?

**Dividing by 10:** If the number's last digit is zero, then it is divisible by 10.

Activity    **Coloring numbers.**

The chart below has the numbers 1 through 100. The numbers colored in red are the numbers divisible by 5, they are lined up nicely in two columns! Color the numbers that are divisible by 9. Do they have an interesting pattern too? How about numbers divisible by 4? Use different colors for a better view of the patterns.

| 1 | 2 | 3 | 4 | 5 | 6 | 7 | 8 | 9 | 10 |
|---|---|---|---|---|---|---|---|---|---|
| 11 | 12 | 13 | 14 | 15 | 16 | 17 | 18 | 19 | 20 |
| 21 | 22 | 23 | 24 | 25 | 26 | 27 | 28 | 29 | 30 |
| 31 | 32 | 33 | 34 | 35 | 36 | 37 | 38 | 39 | 40 |
| 41 | 42 | 43 | 44 | 45 | 46 | 47 | 48 | 49 | 50 |
| 51 | 52 | 53 | 54 | 55 | 56 | 57 | 58 | 59 | 60 |
| 61 | 62 | 63 | 64 | 65 | 66 | 67 | 68 | 69 | 70 |
| 71 | 72 | 73 | 74 | 75 | 76 | 77 | 78 | 79 | 80 |
| 81 | 82 | 83 | 84 | 85 | 86 | 87 | 88 | 89 | 90 |
| 91 | 92 | 93 | 94 | 95 | 96 | 97 | 98 | 99 | 100 |

# Challenge:

1. The number 5241□1 is a number with a missing digit. What digit should be inserted in the blank space so that the resulting number is divisible by 3? How about by 9?

2. The four-digit numeral 2AA2 is divisible by 9. What digit does A represent?

**Prime Numbers**

A prime number is a number that is divisible by just two numbers: 1 and itself.

Example: 2 is a prime number, since it is only divisible by 1 and itself, 2. Likewise, 3 is a prime number, since it is only divisible by 1 and 3. Here are the first six prime numbers: 2, 3, 5, 7, 11, 13.

If a number is not prime, it is called composite. The number 1 is not considered prime or composite; it is a special number in multiplication.

 **History**[5] *Eratosthenes was a famous Greek mathematician who lived a long time ago, around 280 BC. He worked on many topics, answering many interesting questions. In addition to discovering a method to find prime numbers, he measured the Earth's circumference. He is called the father of geography! Here is one final tidbit: Eratosthenes and Archimedes, another great Greek mathematician, were such good friends that Archimedes dedicated a book he wrote to Eratosthenes*[6].

5. Gow, M. (2009). *Measuring the Earth: Eratosthenes and his celestial geometry.* Enslow Publishers, Inc.

6. Chondros, T. G. (2010). *Archimedes life works and machines. Mechanism and Machine Theory,* 45(11), 1766-1775.

# How to Find Prime Numbers: The Sieve of Eratosthenes

Dr. O, Eratosthenes is really cool, but what do you mean by the sieve of Eratosthenes? What does a sieve have to do with prime numbers?

Well, a sieve holds some things back and lets others fall through. With the sieve of Eratosthenes, we block off composite numbers and let prime numbers fall through.

Dr. O, is this a magical sieve you are talking about? How does it work?

**Numbers 2 through 100**

|    | 2  | 3  | 4  | 5  | 6  | 7  | 8  | 9  | 10  |
|----|----|----|----|----|----|----|----|----|-----|
| 11 | 12 | 13 | 14 | 15 | 16 | 17 | 18 | 19 | 20  |
| 21 | 22 | 23 | 24 | 25 | 26 | 27 | 28 | 29 | 30  |
| 31 | 32 | 33 | 34 | 35 | 36 | 37 | 38 | 39 | 40  |
| 41 | 42 | 43 | 44 | 45 | 46 | 47 | 48 | 49 | 50  |
| 51 | 52 | 53 | 54 | 55 | 56 | 57 | 58 | 59 | 60  |
| 61 | 62 | 63 | 64 | 65 | 66 | 67 | 68 | 69 | 70  |
| 71 | 72 | 73 | 74 | 75 | 76 | 77 | 78 | 79 | 80  |
| 81 | 82 | 83 | 84 | 85 | 86 | 87 | 88 | 89 | 90  |
| 91 | 92 | 93 | 94 | 95 | 96 | 97 | 98 | 99 | 100 |

Oh, there is no magic, Arya! I will show you how to find the prime numbers less than 100 using the sieve. First, list all integers 2 through 100 in a table. Think of this table as our sieve.

|    | 2  | 3  | 4  | 5  | 6  | 7  | 8  | 9  | 10  |
|----|----|----|----|----|----|----|----|----|-----|
| 11 | 12 | 13 | 14 | 15 | 16 | 17 | 18 | 19 | 20  |
| 21 | 22 | 23 | 24 | 25 | 26 | 27 | 28 | 29 | 30  |
| 31 | 32 | 33 | 34 | 35 | 36 | 37 | 38 | 39 | 40  |
| 41 | 42 | 43 | 44 | 45 | 46 | 47 | 48 | 49 | 50  |
| 51 | 52 | 53 | 54 | 55 | 56 | 57 | 58 | 59 | 60  |
| 61 | 62 | 63 | 64 | 65 | 66 | 67 | 68 | 69 | 70  |
| 71 | 72 | 73 | 74 | 75 | 76 | 77 | 78 | 79 | 80  |
| 81 | 82 | 83 | 84 | 85 | 86 | 87 | 88 | 89 | 90  |
| 91 | 92 | 93 | 94 | 95 | 96 | 97 | 98 | 99 | 100 |

The first number in the table, 2, is a prime number. Next, we block off all the numbers that can be divided by 2, except for 2. Let's color these numbers by blue. Remember these are composite numbers, since they can be divided by 2.

Then we move on to the next prime number, 3, and block the multiples of 3 in the table.

Oh, I get it! Let's color all the numbers divisible by 3 green.

Some numbers are multiples of both 2 and 3. For example, 6 was shaded in blue already since it is a multiple of 2. You can leave it like that, and not try to shade 6 in green as well!

### Multiples of 2 and 3

|    | 2  | 3  | 4  | 5  | 6  | 7  | 8  | 9  | 10  |
|----|----|----|----|----|----|----|----|----|-----|
| 11 | 12 | 13 | 14 | 15 | 16 | 17 | 18 | 19 | 20  |
| 21 | 22 | 23 | 24 | 25 | 26 | 27 | 28 | 29 | 30  |
| 31 | 32 | 33 | 34 | 35 | 36 | 37 | 38 | 39 | 40  |
| 41 | 42 | 43 | 44 | 45 | 46 | 47 | 48 | 49 | 50  |
| 51 | 52 | 53 | 54 | 55 | 56 | 57 | 58 | 59 | 60  |
| 61 | 62 | 63 | 64 | 65 | 66 | 67 | 68 | 69 | 70  |
| 71 | 72 | 73 | 74 | 75 | 76 | 77 | 78 | 79 | 80  |
| 81 | 82 | 83 | 84 | 85 | 86 | 87 | 88 | 89 | 90  |
| 91 | 92 | 93 | 94 | 95 | 96 | 97 | 98 | 99 | 100 |

Here's what I got, Dr. O!

Arya and Dr. O are blocking the composite numbers by blocking multiples of prime numbers, starting with 2. They blocked the multiples of 2, and then the multiples of 3. The next two prime numbers are 5 and 7. They need to block the multiples of 5 and 7. These numbers are colored in the two tables on the right.

## Multiples of 2, 3, 5

|     | 2  | 3  | 4  | 5  | 6  | 7  | 8  | 9  | 10  |
|-----|----|----|----|----|----|----|----|----|-----|
| 11  | 12 | 13 | 14 | 15 | 16 | 17 | 18 | 19 | 20  |
| 21  | 22 | 23 | 24 | 25 | 26 | 27 | 28 | 29 | 30  |
| 31  | 32 | 33 | 34 | 35 | 36 | 37 | 38 | 39 | 40  |
| 41  | 42 | 43 | 44 | 45 | 46 | 47 | 48 | 49 | 50  |
| 51  | 52 | 53 | 54 | 55 | 56 | 57 | 58 | 59 | 60  |
| 61  | 62 | 63 | 64 | 65 | 66 | 67 | 68 | 69 | 70  |
| 71  | 72 | 73 | 74 | 75 | 76 | 77 | 78 | 79 | 80  |
| 81  | 82 | 83 | 84 | 85 | 86 | 87 | 88 | 89 | 90  |
| 91  | 92 | 93 | 94 | 95 | 96 | 97 | 98 | 99 | 100 |

## Multiples of 2, 3, 5, 7

|     | 2  | 3  | 4  | 5  | 6  | 7  | 8  | 9  | 10  |
|-----|----|----|----|----|----|----|----|----|-----|
| 11  | 12 | 13 | 14 | 15 | 16 | 17 | 18 | 19 | 20  |
| 21  | 22 | 23 | 24 | 25 | 26 | 27 | 28 | 29 | 30  |
| 31  | 32 | 33 | 34 | 35 | 36 | 37 | 38 | 39 | 40  |
| 41  | 42 | 43 | 44 | 45 | 46 | 47 | 48 | 49 | 50  |
| 51  | 52 | 53 | 54 | 55 | 56 | 57 | 58 | 59 | 60  |
| 61  | 62 | 63 | 64 | 65 | 66 | 67 | 68 | 69 | 70  |
| 71  | 72 | 73 | 74 | 75 | 76 | 77 | 78 | 79 | 80  |
| 81  | 82 | 83 | 84 | 85 | 86 | 87 | 88 | 89 | 90  |
| 91  | 92 | 93 | 94 | 95 | 96 | 97 | 98 | 99 | 100 |

The next prime number after 7 is 11. If you look at the table "Multiples of 2, 3, 5, 7", you will notice that all multiples of 11, which are 22, 33, 44, 55, 66, 77, 88, 99, are already shaded in. This means it is time to stop! All un-shaded numbers in the table are prime numbers! They are the numbers the sieve lets fall through. The numbers are:

2, 3, 5, 7, 11, 13, 17, 19, 23, 29, 31, 37, 41, 43, 47, 53, 59, 61, 67, 71, 73, 79, 83, 89, 97

## Prime numbers between 1 and 100

|   | 2 | 3 |   | 5 |   | 7 |   |   |   |
|---|---|---|---|---|---|---|---|---|---|
| 11 |   | 13 |   |   |   | 17 |   | 19 |   |
|   |   | 23 |   |   |   |   |   | 29 |   |
| 31 |   |   |   |   |   | 37 |   |   |   |
| 41 |   | 43 |   |   |   | 47 |   |   |   |
|   |   | 53 |   |   |   |   |   | 59 |   |
| 61 |   |   |   |   |   | 67 |   |   |   |
| 71 |   | 73 |   |   |   |   |   | 79 |   |
|   |   | 83 |   |   |   |   |   | 89 |   |
|   |   |   |   |   |   | 97 |   |   |   |

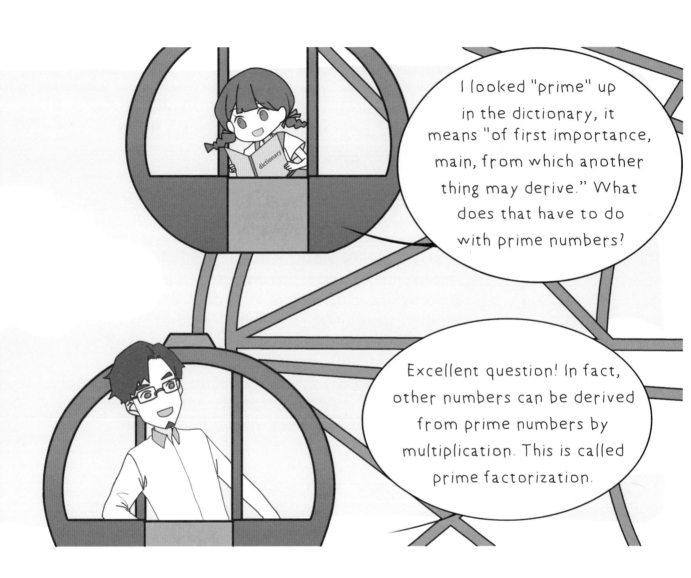

**Prime factorization:** Every positive integer greater than 1 can be written as a product of prime numbers.

**Examples:** 15 = 3 × 5, 18 = 2 × 3 × 3

Here is a method to find the prime factorization of numbers that will be handy when the numbers are larger. Let's find the prime factorization for 60 using this method.

| 60 | 2 |
|----|---|
| 30 | 2 |
| 15 | 3 |
| 5  | 5 |
| 1  |   |

Draw a line next to 60. What is the smallest prime number that divides 60? It is 2. Write 2 on the other side of the line next to 60. 60 divided by 2 is 30: write 30 under 60. Now ask the same question: what's the smallest prime number that divides 30? It is 2 again. So we write 2 on the right of 30. 30 divided by 2 is 15, which we write under 30. The smallest prime number that divides 15 is 3. So 3 goes next to 15, and 15 ÷ 3 = 5 goes under 15. We have come to the end: 5 is a prime number, so we carry 5 to the right of the line, and the factorization is over! The factorization is the product of the prime numbers on the right side of the line: 60 = 2 × 2 × 3 × 5

**Examples:** Find the prime factorization for 90 and for 525.

**Solution:** We apply the method we just learned to these numbers:

| 90 | 2 |
|----|---|
| 45 | 3 |
| 15 | 3 |
| 5  | 5 |
| 1  |   |

The factorization is:

90 = 2 ×3 ×3 ×5

| 525 | 3 | The factorization is: |
|-----|---|------------------------|
| 175 | 5 | |
| 35  | 5 | $525 = 3 \times 5 \times 5 \times 7$ |
| 7   | 7 | |
| 1   |   | |

**Exercise:** Find prime factorizations of 36, 85, and 98.

# Challenge:

30! represents the product of all natural numbers from 1 through 30 inclusive: $1 \times 2 \times .... \times 30$. If the product is factored into primes, how many 5's will the factorization contain?

## An Unsolved Mystery: Goldbach's Conjecture

A conjecture is a statement mathematicians think to be true, but yet they cannot prove it! The Goldbach conjecture says all even numbers greater than 2 can be written as the sum of two prime numbers; for example:

$6 = 3 + 3$

$8 = 3 + 5$

$10 = 5 + 5$, or $10 = 3 + 7$

**Exercise:**

Find two prime numbers that add up to the following even numbers:

12, 14, 46, 58, 60

*Christian Goldbach was a German mathematician who lived from 1690 until 1764. He wrote about the conjecture in his letters to another famous mathematician of the time, Leonhard Euler. Euler said he thought the conjecture must be correct, but he could not prove it.*

*Using computers[8], it has been verified that the Goldbach conjecture is correct for all even numbers up to $4 \times 10^{17}$, on May 26, 2013. This is a number whose first digit is 4, followed by seventeen zeros: 400,000,000,000,000,000.*

7. *Goldbach's conjecture, The Prime Glossary, Chris K. Caldwell, Department of Mathematics and Statistics, The University of Tennessee at Martin. (http://primes.utm.edu/glossary/page. php?sort=goldbachconjecture)*

8. *Goldbach Conjecture Verification, Tomás Oliveira e Silva, Department of Electronics, Telecommunications, and Informatics, University of Aveiro, Portugal. (http://sweet.ua.pt/tos/ goldbach.html)*

## Exercises:

1. The four-digit numeral AB12 is divisible by 4. What do digits A and B represent?

2. What is the smallest positive integer divisible by 2, 3, and 4?

3. There is an even number between 200 and 300 that is divisible by 5 and also by 9. What is that number?

4. N is the 5-digit number 8A65B in which A and B are digits, and N is divisible by 12. What is the smallest number N can be?

# Chapter 5
# NUMBERS WITH SHAPES

## Triangular numbers

A triangular number is the number of dots needed to create a specific kind of triangle. For example, the first 4 such triangles are:

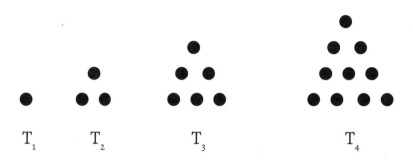

$$T_1 \qquad T_2 \qquad\qquad T_3 \qquad\qquad\qquad T_4$$

**Exercise:** Can you guess what the next triangle of dots will be like? Start with 5 dots on the base, and go up level by level decreasing the number of dots by one at each level.

So what are the triangular numbers? They are the number of dots in the above triangles. Our first triangle is a single dot: we will call this the first triangular number, and write it as: $T_1$ = 1. Here T stands for triangular, and the subscript means we are looking at the first triangular number.

Now let's check out the second triangle: it has 3 dots. So the second triangular number is 3. We write this as: $T_2$ = 3. Similarly, check that $T_3$ = 6 and $T_4$ = 10. Do you notice that the subscript of T equals the number of dots in the base of the triangle?

In summary, the first four triangular numbers are: 1, 3, 6, 10

Can you find the next one, in other words, what is $T_5$ ?

## History

*The Greek mathematician Pythagoras, who lived between 570 - 490 BC (according to the Stanford Encyclopedia of Philosophy), is said to be the first to study triangular numbers. He also studied the mathematics of music. Pythagoras is best known for his famous theorem, the Pythagorean theorem, which states that in a right triangle, the squares of the measurements of the vertical and horizontal sides add up to the square of the length of the third side, which is called the hypotenuse.*

*What is a right triangle? It is a triangle with two sides that are perpendicular to each other, like a and b in the picture below. Side c is the hypotenuse.*

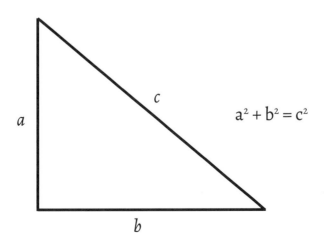

$$a^2 + b^2 = c^2$$

Let's count again, the number of dots in our triangles, but in a specific way. We will start counting from the top dot. For example, for the third triangle, we will count the dots as follows:

$$T_3 = 1 + 2 + 3 = 6$$

Similarly, for the fourth triangle, we have:

$$T_4 = 1 + 2 + 3 + 4 = 10$$

I see a pattern here, Dr. O! The triangular numbers are simply the sum of consecutive integers!

Well done Arya! Can you now find the nth triangular number, $T_n = 1 + 2 + ... + n$, where n is some positive integer?

In summary, here is the secret to computing triangular numbers:

$$T_n = n \times (n + 1) \div 2.$$

Let's verify this formula gives the same triangular numbers we found before: Substitute 2 for $n$ in the formula and we get: $T_2 = 2 \times 3 \div 2 = 3$.

Substitute 3 for $n$ to get: $T_3 = 3 \times 4 \div 2 = 6$.

It certainly works!

# Challenge:

## The Handshake Problem[9]

When the Supreme Court meets, every justice shakes hands with each of the other justices. This has been the tradition for a long time! There are nine justices in the Supreme Court. How many handshakes occur every time they meet?

To answer this question, let's start with assigning a number to each justice, 1 through 9. We will use the table below to keep track of the handshakes!

| Justices | Handshakes |
|:---:|:---:|
| 1 | 8 |
| 2 | 7 |
| 3 | 6 |
| 4 | 5 |
| 5 | 4 |
| 6 | 3 |
| 7 | 2 |
| 8 | 1 |
| 9 | 0 |

Justice number 1, shakes hands with all the other justices, and there are 8 of them. That's why we put 8 in the second column of the table, next to Justice 1.

9. *Supreme Court Handshake, Rhonda Naylor, Illuminations, NCTM*

What about Justice 2? Justice 2 already shook hands with Justice 1. So there are only 7 justices left to shake hands with. We enter 7 handshakes in the table for Justice 2.

Justice 3 has shook hands with Justice 1 and 2, leaving her 6 justices to shake hands with. The pattern emerges! The total number of handshakes is:

$$1 + 2 + 3 + 4 + 5 + 6 + 7 + 8 = 36.$$

SUSTAINED!!

Wait! Isn't 36 also the eighth triangular number, $T_8$?

Arya is correct, and here is the triangle for $T_8$:

## Square numbers

How about we make squares from dots, instead of triangles? Recall that in a square, the height and width are equal to each other. We will call the number of dots needed to make the squares, square numbers, and we will denote them as $S_1$, $S_2$, $S_3$, ..., etc.

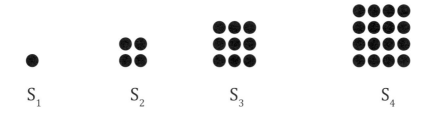

Counting the dots we obtain:

$$S_1 = 1, S_2 = 4, S_3 = 9, S_4 = 16$$

Notice that each number is the square of some number, such as:

$$1 = 1 \times 1$$

$$4 = 2 \times 2$$

$$9 = 3 \times 3$$

$$16 = 4 \times 4$$

Now let's find a general formula for $S_n$: what is the number of dots in a square, if the base has n dots? The answer is:

$$S_n = n \times n$$

There is a special math notation we can use when a number is multiplied by itself:

$$n^2 \text{ means } n \times n$$

Using this notation we can write

$$4 = 2^2$$

$$9 = 3^2$$

$$16 = 4^2$$

and our formula for the $n^{th}$ square number:

$$S_n = n^2$$

**New word**

**Figurate numbers**: These are numbers with form, shape.

# Challenge:

Can a number be both triangular and square? 1 is certainly one such number, since $T_1 = 1$ and $S_1 = 1$. Can you find another number that can be written as $T_n$ and $S_m$, for some integers n and m? (If you find a number that is both triangular and square, draw the triangle and square with that many dots.)

*We can make triangles and squares from dots... what else can we make?*

*We can make ANY shape you would like! How about rectangles?*

Activity | Creating our own numbers with a shape!

Yes, let's try rectangles! A rectangle has a height and width that do not have to be equal. Let's draw rectangles whose heights are twice their width. And let's call the number of dots needed $R_1$, $R_2$, $R_3$,..., etc. Here are the rectangles:

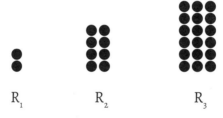

$R_1$ $\qquad$ $R_2$ $\qquad$ $R_3$

Counting the dots, we get:

$$R_1 = 2, \ R_2 = 8, \ R_3 = 18.$$

Now let's find the general formula for $R_n$. There are $n$ dots on the base of the rectangle. Since the height is double the base, there are $2 \times n$ dots on the height. When counting the dots at each level, we will be adding $n + n + ... + n$, precisely $2 \times n$ times. Then the sum is:

$$n \times (2 \times n)$$

By changing the ordering of the numbers, we can write this product as:

$$2 \times n \times n = 2 \times n^2$$

The final answer is:

$$R_n = 2 \times n^2$$

**Exercises:**

1. Create new rectangular numbers where each rectangle height is triple its width. Find the first two rectangular numbers and the general formula for the $n$th number.

2. Arya thinks if we add two consecutive triangular numbers, we get a square number. Do you think she is correct? (Consecutive means the numbers come in succession. For example, 5 and 6 are two consecutive integers; 11 and 13 are two consecutive odd integers; 4 and 9 are two consecutive square numbers.)

# Chapter 6

# WHAT ARE THE CHANCES?

Let's think about some other things that could happen when we roll a die. Let's use the word **outcome** for the number on the top of the die when we roll it. And we will use the word **event** when we have multiple outcomes in mind. For example, having an even outcome when we roll a die is an event, since an even outcome means we either roll 2, 4, or 6.

Here is a question: what is the probability of having an even number as the outcome when we roll a die? Let's write our event as:

Event = "the outcome is even" = {2,4,6}

To find the probability of an event, we do the following:

• Find how many outcomes are contained in the event, in other words, how many times the event can happen;

• Find the total number of outcomes;

• Divide the first number by the second to find the probability.

In the case of the event "the outcome is even,"

• There are 3 outcomes contained in the event (2, 4, and 6)

• The total number of outcomes is 6 (the numbers 1 through 6)

• Therefore the probability of having an even outcome is 3/6 or ½.

New word

**Probability**: When we flip a coin, roll a die, or do something similar where we can't know the outcome in advance, we find the probability of an event by finding the ratio (fraction) of the number of times it can happen to the total number of outcomes.

Dr. O's funny die has six faces, but only three numbers appear on them: 1, 3, 5. Each number appears on two faces. What is the probability that Dr. O rolls a 3?

When we roll the funny die the possible outcomes are: 1, 1, 3, 3, 5, 5. Each number is repeated twice since each number appears on two faces of the die. The number 3 can appear in 2 ways, out of a total of 6 outcomes, so the probability is 2/6, which simplifies to 1/3.

Dr. O, do you know a game we can play with dice?

Sure I do! I call this game Roll for Even!

Here is how Arya and Dr. O play the game. They take turns rolling a pair of fair dice. Once the dice are rolled, they multiply the numbers that are on the top of the dice. If the product is even, Dr. O wins the game. If the product is odd, Arya wins. Let's keep track of the outcomes and the winner:

Game 1: Dr. O rolls 2 and 3. The product is 6, which is even. Dr. O wins!

Game 2: Arya rolls 1 and 5. The product is 5, which is odd. Arya wins!

Game 3: Dr. O rolls 4 and 5. The product is 20, which is even. Dr. O wins!

Arya and Dr. O plays the game ten times. The table below summarizes the results.

|  | Outcomes | Product | Winner |
|---|---|---|---|
| Game 1 | 2 and 3 | 6 | Dr. O |
| Game 2 | 1 and 5 | 5 | Arya |
| Game 3 | 4 and 5 | 20 | Dr. O |
| Game 4 | 3 and 3 | 9 | Arya |
| Game 5 | 5 and 6 | 30 | Dr. O |
| Game 6 | 6 and 1 | 6 | Dr. O |
| Game 7 | 4 and 2 | 8 | Dr. O |
| Game 8 | 3 and 4 | 12 | Dr. O |
| Game 9 | 5 and 1 | 5 | Arya |
| Game 10 | 6 and 2 | 12 | Dr. O |

When we roll two dice there are 36 possible outcomes. You can see these outcomes in the table below, where we write (3,5) to mean the first die shows 3, and the second shows 5. We need to find the product of the values on the dice for each outcome, and count how many of those products are even.

| Outcomes | Product (even or odd) | Outcomes | Product (even or odd) |
|----------|------------------------|----------|------------------------|
| (1,1) | Odd | (4,1) | Even |
| (1,2) | Even | (4,2) | Even |
| (1,3) | Odd | (4,3) | Even |
| (1,4) | Even | (4,4) | Even |
| (1,5) | Odd | (4,5) | Even |
| (1,6) | Even | (4,6) | Even |
| (2,1) | Even | (5,1) | Odd |
| (2,2) | Even | (5,2) | Even |
| (2,3) | Even | (5,3) | Odd |
| (2,4) | Even | (5,4) | Even |
| (2,5) | Even | (5,5) | Odd |
| (2,6) | Even | (5,6) | Even |
| (3,1) | Odd | (6,1) | Even |
| (3,2) | Even | (6,2) | Even |
| (3,3) | Odd | (6,2) | Even |
| (3,4) | Even | (6,4) | Even |
| (3,5) | Odd | (6,5) | Even |
| (3,6) | Even | (6,6) | Even |

Count the evens and odds in the table. There are 27 outcomes that give an even product and only 9 give an odd product! That means the probability that Dr. O wins the game is 27/36 or ¾. Arya wins with probability of 9/36 or ¼.

But why are there so many more even products? The answer is not too difficult to see. The only way to get an odd product is when we multiply an odd number with an odd number. All other arrangements (even times even or even times odd) result in an even product.

Now it's time for snacks!

Let's see how Arya figured out the first bowl gives her a better chance for getting a grape lollipop. There are 3 grape lollipops and 1 orange lollipop in the first bowl. So the probability of picking a grape lollipop while blindfolded is ¾. The second bowl has 5 grape and 3 orange lollipops. Then the probability of picking a grape lollipop from the second bowl is 5/8.

Arya uses a calculator to write these fractions as decimal numbers:

$$¾ = 0.75 \text{ and } 5/8 = 0.625.$$

The first probability is larger! That's why Arya picked the first bowl.

Probability is a relatively recent subject: the mathematicians Blaise Pascal and Pierre de Fermat developed the early foundations of probability in the 1600s. Geometry, on the other hand, was developed two thousand years ago by ancient Greeks! Pascal and Fermat got interested in probability because they were trying to figure out the chances of winning a game of chance. People have been interested in games of chance for a very long time. It is said that the Roman emperor Claudius wrote a book titled "How to Win at Dice" and kept a board in his carriage so that he could play dice games while he was traveling!

Look Arya, look! I am rolling a die and flipping a coin all at the same time!

Now, can you figure out the probability that the coin shows tails, and the die shows 5?

Let's start with writing all possible outcomes when Dr. O rolls the die and tosses the coin. We will use letters H and T for heads and tails. If the coin shows heads and die shows 3, we will write it as: (H, 3). Here are all the outcomes:

(H, 1), (H,2), (H,3), (H,4), (H,5), (H,6), (T, 1), (T,2), (T,3), (T,4), (T,5), (T,6)

Dr. O is asking for the probability of the outcome (T,5), which appears once in our list. There are a total of 12 possible outcomes. The answer is then, 1/12.

**Independent events**: Two events are independent if one event's occurrence does not affect the other event's probability of occurrence.

Here is an example of two events that are **not** independent. We roll a die and let our events be:

Event 1: the outcome is even

Event 2: the outcome is 4

If we think about these events separately then we can tell the first event has probability ½ and the second one has probability 1/6. Now what if after the die is rolled, someone peeks at the outcome and tells us that Event 1 has happened. Will that affect the probability of Event 2?

If Event 1 has occurred, that means the outcome is either 2, 4, or 6. The probability of Event 2, that is the probability that the outcome is 4, is then 1/3.

To summarize, the probability of Event 2 changes from 1/6 to 1/3 if we knew Event 1 has occurred. Therefore, these events are not independent.

## Challenge: A puzzle!

Roll two dice and do the following:

1. Multiply the two top numbers

2. Multiply the two bottom numbers

3. Multiply the top number on the first die with the bottom number on the second die

4. Multiply the top number on the second die with the bottom number on the first die

5. Add all the numbers obtained in steps (1) through (4).

Let's do this once and see what happens!

1.  Say we obtain the following when we roll the dice: the top numbers are 1 and 3.

The product of the top numbers is 3.

2.  The bottom numbers are 6 and 4, and their product is 24.

3.  The top number on the first die is 1, the bottom number on the second die is 4, and their product is 4.

4.  The top number on the second die is 3, the bottom number on the second die is 6, and their product is 18.

5.  The sum of all the numbers is: 3 + 24 + 4 + 18 = 49.

Now you try it with different numbers and see if you notice something strange!

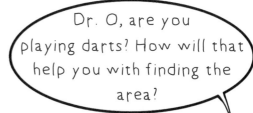

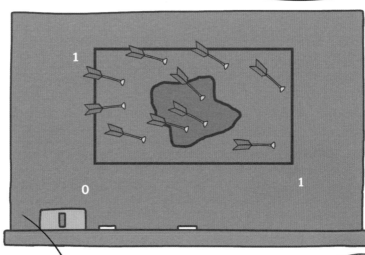

THE END!

# SOLUTIONS

# Chapter 1: Secret Codes

Challenge: How many different Caesar codes can you find?

**Solution:** There are 26 letters in the alphabet. Every shift gives a different code, but when we shift by 26, we get the original alphabet back. So there are 25 different Caesar codes.

**Exercises:**

1.  Encode the message "I came. I saw. I conquered.", using a Caesar code with a key of 5. (Do you know who this quote is from?)

    **Solution:** The encoded message is: N hfrj. N xfb. N htsvzjwji. The quote is from Julius Caesar!

2.  Decode the message "Eqfkpi ku hwp" (Hint: The key is 2.)

    **Solution:** Coding is fun.

# Chapter 2: Number Soup

**Exercises:**

1.  Find the sum of numbers 10 through 20.

    **Solution:** The sum of numbers 1 through 20 is $(20 \times 21) \div 2 = 210$. The sum of numbers from 1 through 9 is $(9 \times 10) \div 2 = 45$. Therefore the answer is $210 - 45 = 165$.

2.  Find the sum of numbers 20 through 30.

    **Solution:** The sum of numbers 1 through 30 is $(30 \times 31) \div 2 = 465$. The sum of numbers from 1 through 19 is $(19 \times 20) \div 2 = 190$. Therefore the answer is $465 - 190 = 275$.

# Chapter 3: What's in an Operation?

**Exercises:**

1. Numbers: 8, 2, 5, 24, 6

   Target: 4

   **Solution:**
   $2 + 5 = 7$
   $8 - 7 = 1$
   $1 \times 24 = 24$
   $24 \div 6 = 4$

2. Numbers: 3, 1, 3, 9, 12

   Target: 14

   **Solution:**
   $9 \div 3 = 3$
   $3 \div 3 = 1$
   $1 + 1 = 2$
   $2 + 12 = 14$

3. Numbers: 3, 11, 2, 3, 6

   Target: 10

   **Solution:**
   $3 + 3 = 6$
   $6 \div 6 = 1$
   $2 - 1 = 1$
   $11 - 1 = 10$

4. Numbers: 6, 1, 4, 21, 7

   Target: 4

**Solution:**

$21 \div 7 = 3$

$6 \div 3 = 2$

$2 - 1 = 1$

$4 \div 1 = 4$

5. Numbers: 5, 3, 3, 3, 12

Target: 9

**Solution:**

$3 + 3 = 6$

$6 - 5 = 1$

$3 \div 1 = 3$

$12 - 3 = 9$

## Challenge:

P, Q represent numbers. P ⊙ Q means $(P + Q) \div 2$. What is the value of 3 ⊙ (2 ⊙ 4)?

**Solution:** 3 ⊙ (2 ⊙ 4) = 3 ⊙ ((2 + 4) \div 2) = 3 ⊙ 3 = (3 + 3) \div 2 = 3

## Challenge:

Does * have an identity element? Recall how we defined this operation: $a * b = a \times (b + 1)$

**Solution:** The answer is no. One might think 0 is an identity element, since

$a * 0 = a \times (0 + 1) = a$. However, $0 * a = 0 \times (a + 1) = 0$, so 0 is NOT the identity element.

**Exercise: (4 numbers only)**

Numbers: 1, 1, 2, 3

Target: 10

**Solution:**

$3 * 2 = 9$

$9 + 1 = 10$

$10 \div 1 = 10$

# Chapter 4: Prime Numbers

**Exercise:** Is 123456 divisible by 2?

Yes, because the last digit, 6, is even.

**Exercise:** Is 123456 divisible by 3?

Yes, because the sum of its digits, 21, is divisible by 3.

**Exercise:** Is 123456 divisible by 4?

Yes, because its last two digits, 56, is divisible by 4.

**Exercise:** Is 123456 divisible by 6?

Yes, because its divisible by both 2 and 3.

**Exercise:** Is 123456 divisible by 9? How about 1234566?

The sum of the digits of 123456 is 21, which is not divisible by 9. Therefore the number is not divisible by 9. The sum of the digits of 1234566 is 27, which is divisible by 9. Therefore 1234566 is divisible by 9.

## Challenge

**Solutions:**

1. From the divisibility rules, a number is divisible by 3 if the sum of its digits is divisible by 3. Let's add the digits except the missing one: $5 + 2 + 4 + 1 + 1 = 13$. Now whatever the missing digit is, when we add it to 13, the sum should

be divisible by 3. For example, the missing digit could not be 1, since then the sum of all digits becomes 14, which is not divisible by 3. The missing digit could be 2, 5, and 8. To be divisible by 9, the sum of all digits must be divisible by 9. Except for the missing digit, the sum of digits was 13. The first number divisible by 9 after 13 is 18. So the missing digit can be 5, since 13 + 5 = 18. The next number divisible by 9 is 27. But we cannot have 27 as the sum of the digits: even if the missing digit was 9 (the largest possible digit), the sum of the digits becomes 13 + 9 = 22, which is less than 27. So the only answer for the second part of the question is that the missing digit is 5.

2. The sum of all digits is 2 + A + A + 2 = 4 + A + A. We can write A + A as 2 times A, or 2 × A. So the sum of all digits is 4 + 2 × A. This sum has to be divisible by 9, for the number 2AA2 to be divisible by 9. Let's check out some of the possible values for A: If A = 1, 4 + 2 × A = 6, which is not divisible by 9. If A =2, 4 + 2 × A=8, which is not divisible by 9. If A = 3, 4 + 2 × A = 10, which is not divisible by 9. We can continue this, or realize a pattern: as A increases, the sum of the digits take on the values 6, 8, 10, 12, 14, 16, 18, 20, 22. The only number in this list divisible by 9 is 18. And the sum is 18 when A = 7. We have our answer! A must be 7.

**Exercise:** Find prime factorizations of 36, 85, 98

**Solution:**

36 = 2 × 2 × 3 × 3
85 = 5 × 17
98 = 2 × 7 × 7

# Challenge:

30! represents the product of all natural numbers from 1

through 30 inclusive: 1 × 2 ×....× 30. If the product is factored into primes, how many 5's will the factorization contain?

**Solution:** The only numbers that have 5 in their prime factorization are: 5, 10, 15, 20, 25, 30. Observe that numbers 5, 10, 15, 20, 30 have exactly one 5 in their prime factorizations, whereas 25 has two. That gives a total of seven 5's.

**Exercise:**

Find two prime numbers that add up to the following even numbers: 12, 14, 46, 58, 60

**Solution:** $12 = 5 + 7$; $14 = 7 + 7$; $46 = 23 + 23$; $58 = 5 + 53$; $60 = 7 + 53$

**Exercises:**

1. The four-digit numeral AB12 is divisible by 4. What digits A and B represent?

   **Solution:** A and B can represent any digit; there is no restriction!

2. What is the smallest positive integer divisible by 2, 3, and 4?

   **Solution:** 12

3. There is an even number between 200 and 300 that is divisible by 5 and also by 9. What is that number?

   **Solution:** 270

4. N is the 5-digit number 8A65B in which A and B are digits, and N is divisible by 12. What is the smallest number N can be?

   **Solution:** N = 80652

# Chapter 5: Numbers with Shapes

**Exercise:** Can you guess what the next triangle of dots will be like? Start with 5 dots on the base, and go up level by level decreasing the number of dots by one at each level.

**Solution:**

## Challenge:

Can a number be both triangular and square? 1 is certainly one such number, since $T_1 = 1$ and $S_1 = 1$. Can you find another number that can be written as $T_n$ and $S_m$, for some integers $n$ and $m$?

**Solution:** Another example is 36. Notice that $S_6 = 36$, and $T_8 = 36$.

## Exercises:

1. Create new rectangular numbers where each rectangle height is triple its width. Find the first two rectangular numbers and the general formula for the nth number.

   **Solution:** The numbers are 3 and 12. The general formula is: $3 \times n^2$

2. Arya thinks if we add two consecutive triangular numbers, we get a square number. Do you think she is correct? (Consecutive means the numbers come in succession. For example, 5 and 6 are two consecutive integers; 11 and 13 are two consecutive odd integers; 4 and 9 are two consecutive square numbers.)

**Solution:** Arya is correct! Two consecutive triangular numbers can be expressed as $T_n$ and $T_{n+1}$. Their sum is

$$T_n + T_{n+1} = [n \times (n+1) \div 2] + [(n+1) \times (n+2) \div 2]$$
$$= [n \times (n+1) + (n+1) \times (n+2)] \div 2$$
$$= [(n+1)(2n+2)] \div 2$$
$$= (n+1)^2$$

which is a square number.

# Chapter 6: What are the Chances?

**The puzzle:**

The sum of the numbers is always 49. Here is why. If you examine a die, you will see that the top and bottom faces always add up to 7. Let's use the letters $a$ and $b$ to denote the top numbers on the dice when we roll them. Then the bottom number corresponding to $a$ will be 7 - $a$, and the bottom number corresponding to $b$ will be 7 - $b$. Here are the calculations:

1. The product of the top numbers: $a \times b$

2. The product of the bottom numbers: $(7 - a) \times (7 - b)$

3. The product of the top number on the first die with the bottom number on the second die: $a \times (7 - b)$

4. The product of the top number on the second die with the bottom number on the first die: $b \times (7 - a)$

We add these using algebra to find

$a \times b + (7 - a) \times (7 - b) + a \times (7 - b) + b \times (7 - a)$

$= a \times b + 49 - 7 \times b - 7 \times a + a \times b + 7 \times a - a \times b + 7 \times b - a \times b.$

Note that all the numbers except 49 cancel out since we are adding opposite numbers, such as $-7 \times b$ and $7 \times b$. Therefore the final answer is 49.

## ABOUT THE AUTHORS

**Arya Ökten** is a PhD student in immunobiology at Yale University, and Dr. O's original student. Arya likes to spend her free time reading books and enjoying good chocolate. **Giray Ökten** is a professor of mathematics at Florida State University. When he isn't at the blackboard, he likes to spend his time listening to classical music and watching film noir movies. Arya and Giray wrote this book over several years based on math workshops they co-taught to students from elementary and middle schools in Tallahassee.

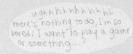